KU-350-635

my favourite

NURSERY RHYMES

Illustrated by: Sophie Fatus Advocate - Art,
Giuliana Gregori Advocate - Art, Siobhan Harrison,
Agnieszka Jatkowska Advocate - Art, Fernando Luiz,
Paul Nicholls Advocate - Art,
Marijan Ramljak Advocate - Art, Emily Smith,
Kanuko Usai and Barbara Vagnozzi.

1
One,

2
two,

3
Three,

4
four,

5
Five,

6
six,

7
Seven,

8
eight,

9
Nine,

10
ten,

Buckle my shoe;

Knock at the door;

Pick up sticks;

Lay them straight;

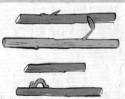

A big fat hen!

Mary, Mary, quite contrary,

How does your garden grow?

With silver bells and cockle shells,

And pretty maids all in a row!

There was a crooked man,
And he walked a crooked mile.
He found a crooked sixpence
Against a crooked stile.
He bought a crooked cat,
Which caught a crooked mouse,
And they all lived together
In a little crooked house.

Three blind mice,
Three blind mice,
See how they run!
See how they run!
They all ran after the farmer's wife,
Who cut off their tails with a carving knife,
Did you ever see such a thing in your life,
As three blind mice?

Little Miss Muffet,
Sat on a tuffet,
Eating her curds and whey.
There came a big spider,
Who sat down beside her,
And frightened Miss Muffet away.

This little piggy went to market,

This little piggy stayed at home.

This little piggy had roast beef,

This little piggy had none.

This little piggy cried, "Wee-wee-wee,"

All the way home.

Jack and Jill went up the hill,
To fetch a pail of water.

Jack fell down and broke his crown,
And Jill came tumbling after.

Little Bo-Peep has lost her sheep,
And doesn't know where to find them.
Leave them alone, and they'll come home,
Bringing their tails behind them.

Humpty Dumpty sat on a wall,
Humpty Dumpty had a great fall.
All the king's horses
And all the king's men
Couldn't put Humpty together again.

I'm a little teapot,
Short and stout.

Here is my handle,

Here is my spout.

When I see the teacups,

Hear me shout,

"Tip me up and pour me out!"

Old Mother Hubbard
Went to the cupboard
To fetch her poor dog a bone.
But when she got there
The cupboard was bare,
And so the poor dog had none.

One, two, three, four, five
Once I caught a fish alive,
Six, seven, eight, nine, ten,
Then I let it go again.
Why did you let it go?
Because it bit my finger so.
Which finger did it bite?
This little finger on the right.

Oh, the grand old Duke of York,
He had ten thousand men.
He marched them up to the top of the hill,
And he marched them down again.

And when they were up, they were up,
And when they were down, they were down,
And when they were only halfway up,
They were neither up nor down!

Little Jack Horner sat in a corner,
Eating his Christmas pie.
He put in his thumb,
And pulled out a plum,
And said, "What a good boy am I!"

Incy Wincy Spider
Climbing up the spout.
Down came the rain
And washed the spider out.
Out came the sunshine
And dried up all the rain,
So Incy Wincy Spider
Climbed up the spout again.